# THE WOMAN SHROUDED IN FLIES

NICHOLAS GRAY

X ______________________________

ISBN-13: 9798747349186

Cover Design by Don Noble

Interior Art by warlocklord

Edited by Lisa Tone

Thank you for creating so many amazing stories that inspired me to read and write. Fear will forever be one of my favorite all-time novels!

"DEATH IS
EVERYWHERE
THERE ARE FLIES ON
THE WINDSCREEN
FOR A START
REMINDING US
WE COULD BE TORN
APART
TONIGHT"

DEPECHE
MODE
'FLY ON THE
WINDSCREEN'

The sun was shining down on the sparkling, dewy freshly-cut grass. It was nine o'clock in Michigan, in the height of summertime, and twelve-year-old Troy's parents were arguing outside the RV. They were trying to get a fire going so they could make pancakes over the campfire. This was their first time attempting campfire pancakes, and it wasn't going well.

Troy wasn't sure what the underlying issue was for their fighting. They wouldn't be at each other's throats if it was really something as minor as pancakes. There had to be something both of them were ignoring that was the real issue, the common denominator as to why they were going at one another. Troy didn't know why they always had to fight, but it drove his anxiety up the wall. They may have been arguing about getting the fire going and making pancakes right then, but there was always another issue at hand. They were always arguing about something menial that didn't matter in the grand scheme of things, and Troy knew it was just a cover for the real reason they were arguing. He was just hoping they wouldn't drag him into their debacle. He hated when they made him pick a side.

He looked out the window of the RV, out towards the woods, trying to see if he could spot anything that would garner his interest and get his attention off the fact that his parents were at each other's throats just a few feet away from him.

What was he looking for to get his attention off his arguing parents? Nothing in particular. It could be a deer, or any animal at that, or other kids adventuring the woods, looking for hidden treasure, like he should be doing right now. Hell, a turd on the ground that was exuding its smelly odor into the air would be something he would be willing to ponder rather than listen to his parents' fight. He would wonder whom took that shit, or what took that shit. It would lead to an array of questions. Like, was it a carnivore, a plant eater, or maybe an omnivore? Hell, guessing which animal took a shit in the camp would be better than listening to his bickering parents. He was hoping something interesting would pop out of the woods and surprise him, anything to keep his mind off his squabbling parents. But he couldn't see anything going on in the woods.

He wished he'd brought something to do, like his Gameboy. Hell, he would even read a book right now if it would distract him from his parents, who were sure enough making a scene outside the RV.

Since they had arrived at Maple Woods RV Park four days ago, Troy's parents had been having nonstop arguments that would make the whole RV Park turn towards them, and it embarrassed the hell out of Troy. His cheeks would go flush, and he would wish he was in a foster home. Anything had to be better than this, he would think. He wished his parents would just stop, but there was no sign of it coming to an end any time soon.

Troy wished they would just be happy, at least for his sake. He knew a ton of kids in his classes who had separated parents that got along for their children's sake, but his couldn't be in the same home with each other without saying something demeaning about the other one. It was a toxic relationship, and he was hoping someone would one day take him away from it all.

He tried to think of a time when they were all happy together, but he couldn't remember such a time. They had always argued. They were either taking turns slinging insults back and forth like a heated tennis match or they were giving each other the silent treatment—which was just as bad, but Troy preferred that over the arguing. The silent treatment only meant that one of the two was going to blow up like an erupting volcano at any minute. It was embarrassing when they turned red in the face and started throwing insults around, letting them fly in all directions, not caring who was in hearing distance.

He had tried to stop their arguing a few times, jumping in the middle of the two and hoping to God they would stop, but it would only escalate the verbal brawl. It would get more heated than before, and the next thing Troy knew, he was a new opponent in the ring.

Troy saw himself as the referee sometimes, but other times he was just a verbal punching bag. Sometimes they would make him choose sides, which was the worst. He hated when that happened. If it were up to him, he would disagree with both of them, because most of the time they were equally in the wrong.

He wanted to just run away. Run as far away as he possibly could until he could no longer hear their insults and never hear it again.

The scent of burning pancake batter hit his nostrils, and his face scrunched up into a grimace. He heard his father yell, "Great! You burnt the pancakes," which was followed by his mother retorting with, "Well, if I didn't have to direct your attention from the slut two campers over, maybe I wouldn't have burnt the fucking pancakes in the first place!"

Tears threatened to fall out of Troy's welling eyes. He was saddened and embarrassed at the same time. He couldn't tolerate this much longer.

He remembered hearing about divorce in class one day when a classmate's parents were going through one. The classmate was feeling low about his parents divorcing, but truth be told, Troy was envious. When Troy learned what a divorce was, he thought he'd discovered an answer to his parents' fighting. He mentioned it once to his mother and got a moldered scolding for it. He wished his parents would get a divorce. It sounded like everything would be much better if they did. They might be able to find someone else, someone who they could stand, and then things would get better. Besides, Troy would receive two Christmases, and that sounded pretty cool to him.

Troy knew they were much happier when they were apart, and it hurt to know that he was probably the glue that kept them together. It was a burden that he carried, but Troy was just a kid.

The worst part of it all was that Troy believed full heartedly he was the reason why they fought. They would fight over who was supposed to pick him up from the karate dojo. They would argue over who he looks more like. They would fight over his grades, his appetite, his weight loss, whether he had depression or not. Whether he should see a therapist. When it came to Troy, his mother wanted what was best for him, but it didn't coincide with what his father thought was best for him. His father believed in discipline, whereas his mother was the type to coddle. They would fight about him constantly, and it made Troy sick to his stomach. He would get physically nauseous, and sometimes he would hide in the restroom and puke his guts out.

He would wonder how the two people who created him could be so agitated at each other and be mad at each other so frequently. He would wonder why they would stay together if they hated each other so much. Wondering these things didn't help much, but he couldn't help it. It's what he thought about a lot.

He sometimes wondered why they even bothered creating him to begin with. Troy figured that if the two of them were happily married before he came along, then it might be safe to say that he himself was the culprit to their arguments.

What was even worse to think about was the dark possibility that maybe they were always like this. Maybe their arguing was bound to happen. They were like oil and water, and they just didn't mix. They were so different in so many ways. Whether it be music, what they liked to eat, they were just so different. Troy didn't understand how they met in the first place.

Maybe misery loves company and seeks out another miserable person to be even more miserable with. They were somehow attracted to each other like magnets. But aren't opposites supposed to attract one another? So, maybe not like magnets.

Sometimes, though, they couldn't be more similar. They were both emotional people, both caring about the other's opinions so much it was irrational, both had a deprecating sense of humor, and they both loved to argue.

So, they would argue all the time, and usually they would fight over Troy, and some days it made Troy wish he was never born.

Other days Troy wished he was dead. Six feet deep in the ground dead. Or burned in a crematorium, where his burdens would burn to ashes. That way his parents could finally split up like they should have done a long time ago. He felt he was the only thing keeping them together, so subtract himself from the mix and they were free to be by themselves and, possibly, happier.

Thoughts of suicide traversed through his mind as his mother walked into the RV and tossed a plate of burnt pancakes onto the table. She then ran to the back room, her face red with rage and her hands clenched into fists. Shortly after, with a similar rage plastered over his face, his father came in, running after his mother. His mother slammed the back-room door of the RV shut and locked it.

Troy's father ran up to the door and began pounding as hard as he could, in hopes that the banging would intimidate her enough to force her into opening the door a smidge. Once she would peer through the door's crack, he would kick it down and force her to meet her problems head on.

"Hey! I'm not done with our little conversation! You can't outrun me forever!" He waited a second for her to respond, and when she didn't, he gritted his teeth and used the side of his fist like a hammer, banging on the door like he was hammering in a nail. "You can't just shove your problems to the side and expect them to just disappear."

Everything from the past wasn't left in the past. No, it was conjured up as if they were doing seances to raise the long dead and forgotten, raising them just to sic the damned souls on one another like some sort of mad voodoo priests battling for voodoo king.

When Troy's mother called his father a "Son-of-a-bitch," at the top of her lungs, Troy couldn't take what was to come. He lived this kind of thing every day. They would verbally jab at each other like pissed off boxers. Each verbal haymaker would attack the opposition with the hopes of a K.O., but both opponents had iron jaws and wouldn't back down.

He couldn't stand their bickering anymore. The fighting was just too much for him today. Troy ran out of the trailer, tears streaming out from his eyes. He heard his father yell out, but the yell wasn't for him. "Open the door, cunt," he screamed at the top of his lungs.

Troy closed his eyes, blinking away the tears, and stormed into the neighboring woods the campground nestled next to. He could barely see where he was going through his watery eyes, but he would see the trees in front of him, and he maneuvered around them.

He ran deeper and deeper into the woods. Branches lashed out against his arms and pulled at his navy blue t-shirt, but he didn't care. He wanted to be as far away from the argument as he possibly could. His mother might open the door, and they may go nose to nose, insulting each other until it took a physical turn, and Troy didn't want to be there for that.

He continued to his way through the trees, running as fast as he could manage. He ran until his foot collided with something hard and caused him to topple and faceplant into the hard earth beneath him. His knee hurt from the collision it made with the woodland floor. He rubbed his bruising kneecap, hoping it would make the pain go away, and though it didn't accomplish that, it did relieve the pain a smidge.

Troy wiped his eyes with his forearm, clearing his vision enough to get a good look at the nasty raspberry growing on his kneecap. "Crap," he said in a frustrated tone—"Crap," the extent of cursing he was willing to go. He could never risk his parents overhearing him saying something like 'shit' or 'fuck', but he needed to express in word the pain that coursed through his knee at that moment. If they did catch him cursing, at least it was a word like 'crap' instead of something much worse. Something he would surely get a whipping for.

Troy picked himself up, rubbing the dirt off himself, then turned around to see what he had stumbled on. He was expecting a tree root, or possibly an animal of some sort, or maybe a kid from the campground with his leg stuck out to trip him. He didn't expect to see what laid in the small clearing before him.

Fright flooded into him like a bursting dam allowing water on a populace of people, making him choke on his words as though water was filling up his lungs.

The woman who lay splayed out on the woodland floor had her eyes closed shut. At first, Troy thought she was asleep, but when his eyes inevitably made their way to the woman's breast, he realized there was no rise and fall to her chest. She was clothed in a gray V-neck shirt that was lifted over her breasts to reveal a white bra, which was crooked and out of place. The woman's blue jeans and white underwear were pulled down to her ankles, revealing the dark patch of hair in between her thighs.

Troy's heart raced, and he felt like he was going to pass out. He was in a fight or flight mode, but there was nothing to fight. Unless there was. Something had to have killed this woman. At that moment, Troy knew he had to get out of there. Out of the woods before a possible monster came out of the shrubs to end his short, pitiful life because his dumb ass had stumbled over the woman that he—or it—just had killed.

But before Troy could take off and leave the half-nude dead woman in the dust, the breeze blew by, wafting the scent of the woman into Troy's wide-open mouth. His panting was the reason for his mouth being open, and Troy wished the malodorous scent didn't hit his tongue, but it did. It did and he could now taste and smell the death in the air.

That's when he noticed the flies.

The swarm of flies flew around the body as if protecting their dinner. They were angry at him for disturbing their lunch and for disturbing their young. Troy noticed the whitish yellow maggots inching along around the semi-bloated body, digging into her flesh and innards as if she were carrion. But she was more than just some roadkill on the side of the road. She was a person, a beautiful human being … at least she was once upon a time.

The flies buzzed, as if yelling at him to leave, claiming her as their own. She belonged to the flies now, Troy realized in a sick moment. He could feel bile rising in his throat, and he doubled over and lurched up last night's dinner. More food for the flies' hungry young, Troy sickly thought. The thought of the flies and maggots feasting on his half-digested meal made him heave once more, upchucking what little was left in his belly.

He wiped the vomit from his mouth with the back of his forearm and tried not to look at the woman on the ground in front of him. But that was damn near impossible. You see, the woman's half-naked body, even in the state it was in, aroused him. Her big breasts and figure, even though bloated, looked really appealing to the pre-teen boy.

He instantly knew that what he was feeling was wrong, but he couldn't help it. He had never seen a naked woman up close like this before. He was only twelve years old, so seeing a stunning nude woman lying just inches away from him made his body stiffen up. But the fear of it all was residing in him as well and slowly crawling to the surface. The competing emotions were hard for him to sort out.

It bothered him, and he struggled with what he should be doing with himself at that moment. Part of him—the sane part, he figured—wanted to bolt back to the campground and leave this whole mess behind him and forget it even ever happened—if his mind would allow him to forget. The other part of him wanted to see more of the exposed woman. The curiosity in him needed to know what she felt like and what he would feel like inside the woman.

Troy's hand reached into his shorts, and he began to stroke himself.

He wasn't just pleasuring himself because a beautiful woman laid sprawled out only a few inches away from him, although it was a big part of the reason. He was stressed out about the scene he had left in the RV, where his parents bickered and fought with one another. The stress of his home life mixed with the encounter with this beautiful dead woman was just too much for him. He miserably knew he was probably a sick fuck for doing this, but he needed the stress to go away, and the only way his young mind new how to release that sort of tension was to masturbate. To release all the stress harbored inside of him and expel the negative energy for an exchange of serotonin equivalent of nirvana.

As Troy stroked himself, he looked at the dead woman on the ground. The dead woman's round breasts were white as snow. Dead pale. The type of complexion a person in a coffin would have.

He shrugged the thought of her being dead away and just focused on her sexual attributes.

She was a beautiful woman, and Troy doubted he would ever be able to do this in front of someone that gorgeous again. Her long dark hair was caked with dirt, but Troy wanted to run his fingers through it, twirl it with his finger like one would twirl a spaghetti noodle with a fork. His eyes went down to her dark, hairy crotch. and he stroked a little faster.

That's when the body jerked.

Troy was about to climax, toes curling in his shoes as he felt it all coming up, when the woman's head jerked to the side to face him. The dead woman's eyes were open in a fraction of a millisecond. There was seemingly no transition. One second her eyes were closed, the next they were open. Her eyes were that of a dead woman's, foggy white, but her dead stare looked too alive for Troy, and he immediately stopped masturbating and let out a frightened yell.

He fell backwards then, kicking his legs out and propelling himself backwards as he did an odd crab walk away from the dead woman. But Troy wondered if she were really dead now.

Despite the way she looked, looking dead as a cadaver should, her eyes had opened, her head had turned, and she had looked at him. It just didn't seem right. Dead people don't just open their eyes and stare at people, do they?

Troy's body was tremoring with fear. He knew what he was doing was wrong, but his body betrayed his first instinct to run, and now he was in a predicament his mind didn't know what to do about. He kept looking at the dead woman with his frightened eyes, trying to think. Then he suddenly thought about some of the true crime documentaries his mother and father would watch when they thought he was asleep in bed—when he was really peering out his door to the living room, sneaking a peek.

The scenes he would watch were not right for a developing mind like his own, but he enjoyed watching them, and so far, no one had caught him. He sometimes wished he could plop on the couch with his parents and share their investment in the crime drama with them, but he knew it would probably start another argument. That was the only time his parents really got along, and him trying to join in would probably just ruin it for them.

What went through Troy's brain was something he had heard on those true crime dramas. He'd learned the body could twitch, spasming even after death. It was just a process of death. The muscles would jerk and tremble like certain lizards' tails. Human bodies spasmed for multiple reason, one being muscle memory, the other being the expelling of gasses.

But Troy knew this was neither of those things.

The way the woman's head snapped directly towards him and her eyes stared daggers into him, well, it just told him she had intentionally looked towards him in the middle of his dirty deed.

Either this woman was alive and maybe this whole thing was a prank, which would be really embarrassing, or she was some sort of zombie, coming alive to pick at his mind, and not in a good way. If she were a brain eating zombie, then he was in big trouble.

Either option spelled problems for him.

His rational mind was split between the two options, but he was leaning towards her being a reanimated corpse, even though he knew that was the least believable option. But he could see decomposition on her body, which definitely detailed her being dead. He guessed a good makeup artist could come up with this effect, but he wasn't important or famous enough to be pranked in such a manner. And he also knew it was impossible to replicate that maggots that were feasting in her insides. Everything about the woman screamed dead, yet there she was, staring up at him with malice in her dead eyes. Then there was the smell that wafted off her. Living people didn't expel that type of smell. Decaying corpses did. That's exactly what she was, and he knew it to be true, but Troy's rational brain just couldn't wrap around this impossibility before his very eyes.

As his rational mind tried making sense of the scene before him, something else happened that he wasn't expecting, even from a corpse that was seemingly staring up at him and defying the laws of logic anyways.

The woman's right arm moved across her body and rested on her left side. Then, with both arms, she pushed her herself up. A gushy snapping sound followed by the sound of ripping flesh snapped Troy out of his rational thinking and left him stunned, mouth hanging agape, at what was happening before his very eyes. He was like a deer caught by a vehicle's high beams. He didn't understand what he was seeing and was trying to comprehend it. He was paralyzed by fear. He couldn't move. His brain took that time to assess the situation, though, and on the top of the list of things that made sense to do was run. Run like he was being chased by a bear. But fear was entrapping him, cementing his feet to the woodland floor like he had cinderblocks for shoes.

All he could do was recoil as the woman slowly crawled towards him.

Troy looked at the woman and noticed she had left the lower half of her body behind like it was some sort of detachable figurine. She was nothing but a torso with arms and a head with a gnashing maw, which was gurgling up a mixture of vomit and maggots as she approached him. The lower part of her upper half dragged intestines that were visibly being chewed on by a mixture of bugs—but mostly maggots—feeding on her insides like she was some sort of human body buffet.

By the time Troy finally had the gall to attempt to run away, it was far too late.

Troy took a running stride to the left of the crawling, maggot infested woman, but she was quicker than he could have possibly imagined. She wouldn't let him escape that easily.

Her grab for the boy's ankle was swift, causing him to trip, which in turn sent him tumbling to the ground and slamming face-first into the dirt. Troy's head was spinning, and his mouth was filled with grassy dirt. The fall knocked the air out of his chest, and he wheezed in the dirt in his mouth, which caused him to cough and wheeze more to the point where his eyes started to water. He spat the earth from his mouth and looked up. His eyes were fighting to see through the tears, but as soon as his vision cleared, he saw the lower half of the woman's body lying a mere inch away from his face. The legs began to jerk and twitch, as if it had electric jolts surging through it, forcing the legs to kick out and spasm, kicking dirt this way and that way. Troy recoiled, instinct telling him to move backwards, away from that thrashing body, but that's when a hand grabbed his shoulder and pinned him to the grass.

As Troy was forced to the ground, his face was turned upwards, leaving him looking at the tree canopies and the gloomy, clouded gray sky. Soon, the sky was eclipsed by the maggot infested woman, who, even though half of her was at his feet, towered over him menacingly.

The reanimated woman's jaw unhinged, and her maw became twice as large. Inside her mouth crawled hundreds of yellowish-white maggots that squirmed with delight. They were feasting on her half rotten tongue.

Troy screamed at the same time the woman's gagging and choking commenced, and he found out fast that it wasn't a good time to scream. Puke mixed with maggots flooded his face, entering his mouth. The taste was horrendous and unbearable. He immediately went to heave and upchuck, wanting to projectile vomit skyward to cleanse himself of the horrible taste of maggots and puke juice that filled his mouth, but the woman quickly covered his nose and mouth with her hands, making sure he ingested the regurgitation—like a mother bird feeding its hatchlings, but much more forceful.

Troy fought against her, but to no avail. He felt the vomit and maggot concoction shoot up his nose, but it had no way to escape, so it slunk back down into his mouth, causing him to retch again. But the woman wouldn't allow her revolting meal to be wasted, rejected like an ungrateful child spitting out a well-prepared meal that took hours to create.

Without any way to expel the maggot vomit smoothie that was forced inside him, he was finally forced to swallow it. It was the only way to breathe again. He didn't know why this was the case. For all he knew, the woman may just pin him down and let him suffocate to death.

It was the vilest thing he had ever experienced in his life. The chunky bits inside the vomit, mixed with the squirming maggots, made it difficult to force down, but somehow, Troy was able to get it down.

As the vomit maggot concoction went down his throat, his body decided the vile brew wasn't meant to be swallowed, and it all came right back up. The vomit wanted to eject out his nose and mouth, stinging his sinuses with the acidic smell of puke, but with the woman's impossibly strong grip over his mouth and nose, it was impossible to rid of the vomit mix inside him.

Two minutes went by of Troy drowning on maggot infested bile before everything began to dim. Life was fading to black. Troy wondered for a brief second if this was what life after death was: nothingness. He wondered if he would fade into nonexistence, like a never-ending dreamless sleeping state. It terrified Troy, but at the same time, he began to welcome death. The pain of being alive, drowning on maggoty vomit and living with parents who fought all the time, well, it didn't exactly make for a life he wanted to live.

Troy allowed his eyes to slowly shut as the darkness took over.

***

Troy's parents were in a yelling match, shouting at each other from two different closed off rooms. Stinging name callings went back and forth, and Troy's father'd had just about enough of it. He called her a cunt after she called him a pencil dick, which found his soft underbelly, his weak spot. He knew he could never satisfy her in bed, and he wondered if that was the whole reason for this fight. Was his sexual inadequacy the reason for her hatred towards him? No. The reason she was mad at him had nothing to do with his poor attempts at pleasuring her. It was about Troy. It's always about fucking Troy, he thought. This fight was whether Troy needed to see a psychiatrist or not. The answer for her was clear. She wanted him to seek help. But Troy's father didn't want his perfectly capable son to have his head examined and experimented on like some sort of lab rat. No son of his would be someone's guinea pig.

He knew what it was like to be fucked up on prescription medicine. He had been an addict for a few years before Troy was born. He'd loved his Percocet—or as he liked to call them, his perkies—due to the fact that he was always happy when he was high on them. He quit them when he met the woman of his dreams. But little did he know that his dream girl would soon turn into a nightmare.

Things went well for him and his woman of his dreams for two whole years. He proposed to her, and then they got married, and immediately after that, she became pregnant with Troy. That's when things really went downhill. Troy's mother had become infatuated with the baby, as most mothers do when they bear a child. Troy's father, however, felt like the love they shared drifted towards Troy; the love that should have been for him was now given to the boy. It was like there wasn't enough love in her heart to be shared with two individuals. He started to grow a disdain for Troy as the distance between him and the love of his life turned into a gorge. He still wanted what was best for his son, but he didn't really want much to do with him.

Then the day came when he found out his wife of ten years was having an affair with another man. It crushed his heart when he found out through a confession from her that she had cheated on him for three years prior and wanted a divorce. Ever since then, he'd felt inadequate. Like he wasn't enough. Her plan was to run off with this other man and live a better life. But Troy's father wasn't having it.

The only reason they were still together was because he threatened to take Troy away from her, which was enough to scare her back into the relationship. She couldn't live without her baby, and she didn't want to share him. She wanted him all to herself.

So, for a few years now, they were a bickering couple that would argue like this to no end, no matter where they were or who was around. It was like something possessed them to argue. It could be about little things or big things. The menial things that didn't really matter would start the arguments, but they would escalate to other things.

Today was about Troy's health and wellbeing, which he believed was fine and nothing to worry about. The only thing wrong with Troy was that he was too much like his mother: soft. It was annoying that Troy wasn't into the same sports as he was in. There is no way, NO WAY you could come from my loins, he would reference. It was a quote from a classic movie he and his dad used to watch when Troy's father was younger. Movies like Smokey and the Bandit and the time spent watching it with his father were some of the greatest moments in his life. It molded him into the man he was today. Troy had no interest in movies like that. He would rather watch horror movies instead of satirical comedies from way back.

Troy's father didn't understand his son's fascination with horror movies. What was the point of watching a film that would scare you? It didn't make sense to him. Sometimes he wished his son was more like himself and less like a freak. He wished his son would grow a pair, but he was beginning to feel like that day would never come. A real man would take an offered beer without any hesitation, but when he offered his son a beer, trying to have a father to son moment, Troy ran to his mother and snitched on him. What the Hell is that shit? he thought. That had started a huge pandering he didn't want or need at the time.

He sometimes wondered if fighting over Troy was even worth it. In the end, though, it wasn't really about Troy and what he thought was best for the kid. It was about getting his way, which usually happened to be the opposite of that of his wife.

He also got a little something out of arguing with his wife. Sometimes he agreed with her on all accounts, but he would play devil's advocate just for the sake of arguing. He loved getting a rise out of her. In some sick, perverse way, it sort of turned him on. He couldn't rationalize it, but seeing his wife aggravated gave him a kind of sick pleasure. His cock would get hard, and sometimes he thought about forcing it into her and having his way with her, but he never crossed that line. With her.

Maybe it was because he got off more on the arguing itself than sex. He really couldn't explain it. He would imagine punching her in the mouth until her teeth popped out and blood would flow down her chin from the impact, then he would imagine impaling her on his shaft and forcing her to like it.

Troy's father was a sick man, and he knew this to be true. He knew he was sick when he was a teenager and thought about violent things he wanted to do to girls. But he was always terrified of the consequences that came with it. He was just as sick as most other men, he thought. But most men didn't harbor a devil in them like Troy's father did.

Sometimes he had to release some of the anger and perverse thoughts he had, and masturbation just didn't cut it. A couple of nights ago, he woke up late in the night and tried to get his wife to have sex with him. But she wasn't having it. She despised him and didn't want to have sex with him ever again.

So, being sexually frustrated and angry at his wife, the now wide-awake man with a caged inner demon decided to go for a walk to smoke a cigarette, even though the campground explicitly said smoking wasn't allowed on the premises.

He walked around the campground, aimlessly traversing his way past dark, unlit campers, until a young brunette woman caught his attention. She was walking away from her campsite and toward the restrooms. She was an attractive woman. He stared at her. His dark gray hoodie and black pajama bottoms almost made him invisible in the dark of night, and she was oblivious to his prying eyes undressing her. The woman carried a flashlight, which was aimed in front of her, and not once did it swing around to get a look at him.

The restrooms were at the brim of the campsite, near where his RV resided. He followed the girl to the restrooms, staring at her backside the whole time, but at a good enough distance to where she couldn't feel his eyes on her. She entered the lady's restroom, and he waited for her just outside. No one was up right now, and crickets serenaded the crisp, summer's night air.

When the woman exited the restroom, her flashlight flicked on and beamed into the darkness.

She wasn't prepared for the wallop that connected with her face. She fell to the ground and let out an audible umph, the only noise she could make with the air whooshing out of her lungs all at once. Blood filled her mouth as Troy's father's fantasy was coming true. She had bitten down hard on her tongue. Once the air came back to her, she went to scream as loud as she could, but it never escaped from her bloody mouth.

He saw she was about to scream and dropped on her, mounting her. His knees clamped down on her wide hips, and he started raining down blows to her face with the quickness of a professional boxer. The girl whimpered while the beating commenced, but her eyes eventually fluttered shut, and she passed out.

He thought he may have killed the girl right there and then, which would have ruined his plans. He wanted to rape this woman, but he was no necrophiliac. Then he started to ponder what intercourse with a dead woman would feel like.

He shook off the thought and then took a step back to evaluate his victim. Her mouth was agape, and she was letting out bubbled, raspy wheezes. He could see that her front four top teeth were missing. Probably swallowed them, he thought. Troy's father looked both directions, and when he didn't see a soul in sight, he knew the coast was clear. He picked the girl off the ground and threw her over his shoulder. He was ready to delve deeper into depravity.

Since everyone at the campground was asleep, no one noticed Troy's father carrying the passed-out woman to a clearing in the woods that bordered the campground. He took her to a clearing where no one would hear or see his evil intentions.

He plopped the woman onto the ground and examined her. She was gorgeous, and his cock was ready. His cock was as hard as concrete.

He dropped down to the woodland floor and began pulling her pants and panties down. Once they were down enough to where he could slip himself inside her, he lowered his pajama bottoms and got on his hands and knees and hovered over the woman, darkening her figure with his own shadow.

"This will be over quick, I promise," he said, smiling gleefully.

Then he raped her unconscious body. He was rough with her. He created slapping noises with every thrust, and his grunts increased in volume, but there was no one around to hear the assault taking place.

He was startled to see the woman's eyelids fluttering open, her eyes rolling around in their sockets, trying their darndest to focus on any of her surroundings. He averted his eyes from the semi-conscious woman and instead focused on her body, not wanting his hard on to go to waste, especially since time was of the essence. He knew he didn't have long before she gathered her senses and attempted to fight back, or worse, got a good look at him. He worried she would identify him to the police and he would have to face the consequences for what he was doing. He didn't give her much of a chance at the restrooms to ID him, but now she could look while he was inside her and he would have no choice but to end her life, and he didn't view himself as a murderer. Not yet, at least.

His thrusts became faster and faster, and his toes began to curl. With one last hard push inside of her, he began to buckle. He shut his eyes tight, squeezing her right breast hard with his left hand, and emptied himself within the woman. He heaved in a few pants and smiled. But his smile dissipated when he looked up from his cock and into the eyes of the woman.

The woman was fully conscious now and giving him an icy, daggered stare. She didn't say a word, though, and they stared at each other for what felt like an eternity.

His face turned to one of concern and fear, fear for his own life. She had obviously gotten a good look at him now. She was taking in his features and saving them to her memory, storing them away for the cops when she told them what he'd done to her.

He was fucked.

Sure, he could claim it wasn't him, but they wouldn't take his side, especially once rape kits were implemented. He would be fucked. Life ruined. He would go to jail, and that would be that.

Her face was one of boiled hatred. He knew she wouldn't enjoy what he did to her, but he wasn't expecting this. He truly thought he could get away with it. She'd seemed to awaken from her passed-out state relatively quickly, and she didn't even make a peep, just allowed him to finish inside her without letting out so much as a yelp.

Why didn't she make a noise? He kept wondering why, rolling it over in his mind over and over again. He began to wonder if it was because he was terrible at intercourse. Maybe she could barely feel his small penis inside of her. He wasn't big enough to make her moan, whether from ecstasy or pain. He just wasn't good enough.

The thought of not being sexually satisfying to this woman began to turn his face red with rage. His once fearful expression expired and was replaced with one of malice. He let go of her breast, brought both his hands to her throat, and began to squeeze.

He didn't know if his hands were shaking from exertion or from pure, unadulterated anger. His eyes became as bloodshot as hers, except her eyes were popping out of her skull. Her tongue bulged out of her mouth as she began to ache for oxygen. She tried to kick her legs and scratch at him, but she wasn't succeeding at freeing herself.

Troy's father was no longer looking at the woman he'd just knocked out and raped out in the woods by the campground. The woman's face morphed into his wife's, and this made him even angrier. He wanted to choke the bitch out even more than before. It was no longer about the woman beneath him. To him, it was about revenge on the woman back in his RV. It was all her fault. The reason he was even raping this woman in the woods was her doing. If she would have put out more, maybe he wouldn't feel sexually frustrated. If she just loved him as much as he loved her, maybe he wouldn't be so angry all the time. It was all her fault. He couldn't be faulted for this woman's rape and murder because, in his eyes, he wasn't in control of his emotions. It was the bitch back at the camper that made me do this, he thought. If she would have made love to him more, and only him, then he would never feel these urges.

But that was all a lie, and deep down, he knew it, but in that moment, all he could see was red. All he could think of was the wrongs his wife had done to him.

So he continued to strangle the woman.

By the time his anger dissipated, it was far too late for the woman. His hands were locked around her neck like a dog clasping its jaws on a squirming squirrel. But she was no longer alive. He couldn't feel thumping in her chest indicating a heartbeat. He had rung the woman's neck with his bare hands, breaking her trachea without even knowing it. He had killed her.

His hands began to shake uncontrollably. He brought his hands up to his face, the same hands that had just murdered a complete stranger in the woods. He had a week and a half to go before they would leave the campground and be far away from this place. He knew he had to play it cool.

He kept rolling the situation over in his mind as he picked himself up off the dead woman. His hands were still trembling as he looked from his palms to the woman on the ground before him. He quickly went over to a nearby bush and vomited up the hotdogs they had made over the campfire for lunch. Whipping his mouth dry of the hotdog slush that he had just thrown up, he looked back at the girl and realized how much of his DNA was around this crime scene. He knew right there and then that he needed to leave, leave as soon as possible, before he left more evidence of his presence at the scene of the crime.

His mind reeling from what he had just done, he took off running out of the woods and back to the RV.

Now, here he was, yelling with his wife yet again about something irrelevant in the grand scheme of things. The elation of raping and murdering that woman, replacing the woman's face with his wife's, hadn't lasted long. He suspected his wife knew something was up. She must have noticed him missing that night. He could have gotten up to use the restroom, which was an adequate excuse. Except he was gone for almost an hour and their camper had a bathroom built inside of it, so there was no reason for him to exit the RV to go use the restroom.

She also had to know something was up due to the fact that there was a person camping on the other end of the Campground who had freaked out about his missing fiancé the day after Troy's father did that dirty deed. The man with the missing fiancé was wandering the campground screaming for her and approaching each RV, asking if people had seen her and even showing everyone a picture of her.

When he approached Troy's family's camper, Troy's father coldly told the man that he had no idea where his fiancé was and even had the gall to say that maybe she ran off with another man. The guy frantically said that there was no way she would do such a thing, to which Troy's father replied with, "Maybe you weren't satisfying her needs," which angered the man. The man went to ask, "What's that supposed to mean?" but was cut off by Troy's father slamming the camper's door shut. The man banged his fists on the door a few times but eventually left, probably realizing it was a waste of his time, time that he could be spending looking for his lost fiancé.

Maybe Troy's mother was piecing together the puzzle and coming to a sick conclusion. The fight they were currently having may be a front. Maybe she was scared for her life and was pretending to be frustrated about their crumbling marriage so she could lock herself in the back bedroom away from the monster that was Troy's Father.

Neither parent was nervous about their missing son, they believed there was more important things at hand. They couldn't get past their bitter and petty ways to sit down together and wonder where the Hell their son ran off to. Troy's father shrugged the thought of his son to the side. He figured he was out exploring the campsite or trying to get it on with a girl his age. He didn't really think his son was into girls, but he so desperately wished his son was. Troy's father believed that if Troy was to ever get laid, then maybe they would have something more to talk about. They were complete opposites, and Troy's father hated that.

But in reality, they had more in common then he would ever know.

Troy's father banged on the door, demanding that his wife come out and talk to him face to face. She yelled back a "Fuck you," that made his skin boil. He tried to think about the strangled woman he'd raped to calm and relax him, like he had been doing up to now, but it just wasn't cutting it.

"Hey. Bitch," Troy's father yelled. Calling her a bitch, a whore, a cunt and a slew of other things was more normal than him saying her actual name. "Open the goddamned door before I break it down!"

"You wouldn't dare," she yelled back, "You know how much it would cost to repair it!"

Troy's father knew exactly how much it would cost to replace the door, but he didn't give a damn. It was just a lousy door that was separating him from her. But the more he thought about it, the more he knew she was right. They weren't exactly in a financial situation to be destroying the RV. They had money, but not enough to spare for repairs.

He growled and went to bang on the door again, but he held his fist an inch away from the door and instead yelled out to her, telling her she had five minutes before he was barging in.

She didn't reply, and that made him even more upset, which was almost impossible to do. Not being acknowledged was a pet peeve of his. He hated it when people didn't reply, especially when he asked them a question.

"Fucking answer me, bitch!"

A solid ten seconds went by without a reply. His hands clenched into fists, and he was about to yell an obscenity when a shrill scream came from within the bedroom.

Troy's father at first thought she was screaming for help, like she was hoping the neighboring campers would hear her and come to investigate and possibly intervene, saving her from him, the abusive husband. It wouldn't be the first time she had done that. But that thought passed quickly. The scream went on and seemed like one of all-encompassing fear.

He was suddenly worried for his wife. He loved the woman, at least he thought he did, and that was enough for him to be concerned for her wellbeing.

He attempted to open the door again, turning the knob over and over, but to no avail. The door wouldn't budge.

He went to break it down, thought for a moment about the cost to repair the door, then called out to her instead.

"Sweety," he said with a concerned but panicked voice, "I need you to open the door for me or else I can't help you!"

Another shrill scream reverberated off the tinny walls of the RV, which made him drop the concern for the door.

He tried his shoulder first, but after throwing himself against the door and having it hurt like hell, he remembered hearing on TV that using your legs to knock a door down was the way to go, since it strained you less than shouldering it. So, he began to kick the door. At first it didn't do much. The door was a sturdy one, but it wasn't a match for Troy's Father's strength.

The door finally splintered, then cracked, then eventually ripped from its hinges and toppled over, revealing a horrid scene.

His wife was sprawled out on the floor with some sort of dark, fuzzy entity on top of her. At first, he thought his eyes were playing tricks on him. It looked kind of like the television static he would see on the old television sets he watched in his younger days. When he changed the station to one that had nothing on it, he would get the white and black fuzz followed by a static noise. But the noise he heard now wasn't like that. The buzzing was a cacophony that roared in his ears. It encompassed the bedroom and made him falter just a bit. He retreated half a step and stared in awe at what was in front of him.

In front of him was not an entity made out of static, but of flies. It was the sound that tipped him off. A memory from his childhood popped into his mind.

When he was eight or nine years old, he had found a dead squirrel on his walk to the school bus. The thing had been infested with maggots and had flies buzzing all around it. Its rotting carcass steamed up a smell that was like poison to his lungs. He had coughed, then ran past it without a second thought.

Why this memory came to his mind was beyond his him. But even though he had answered the question of what was making the buzzing sound, it only left more questions for him to decode. Like, why were there so many flies in the room? Sure, food going bad could be an answer to his question, but in the bedroom of all places? That wasn't where they kept their food.

Troy's father had never seen so many flies in one place before. It was like seeing a huge shoaling of fish swimming around in the ocean, but much smaller and condensed into a small room in a RV. His mind was having a hard time deciphering who it was underneath the cloak of flies, but he didn't have to wonder for long.

Underneath the veil of flies was a person, and that person was turned towards him, staring at him with an intensity to his glare. The flies cloaking the man began to shift, clearing way to reveal a face on the entity's body. When they cleared, Troy's father instantly knew who was under the heap of flies. It was his son.

Troy winked at his father, then turned to his mother and leaned down. What Troy's father saw next made him want to yack up everything he had eaten from the last week.

Troy's mouth started to stretch impossibly, becoming a large maw. In a split of a second, flies were whizzing out of his mouth and flying directly into his wife's opened, awe-struck mouth.

The flies pelted at her uvula, then collided with the back of her throat. The force of the flies passing through her lips was like that of a firehose. Troy's father was bewildered as he watched his wife attempt to close her mouth. When that didn't work, she tried to vomit it all back up, but instead she began making choking noises from the vomit shooting up her throat but not being able to project outward because of the flies forcing it back down her burning throat.

Troy's father watched in horror as the flies flew into her. He was paralyzed, partly because he didn't want to end up in her position as well.

Then, his horror grew tenfold as he watched her belly distend. She became pregnant with the flies entering her stomach.

Eventually, the fear began to subside, being replaced by rage once again. He was about to jump at his son, tackle him to the ground to save his wife from the abuse she was suffering, when he began to hear a tear, like Velcro slowly being pulled apart. He looked at his wife's bulging figure and saw bloody stretch marks covering her middle and bloody streaks pressing out of newly formed tears.

His fear abruptly returned. His feet felt like they were encapsulated in giant ice blocks. He continued to listen to the tearing noise, watching her stomach distend to an unimaginable girth.

Finally, a deep gurgling noise came from his wife, and in a blink of an eye, her belly exploded, sending chunks of her flying all over the room. He flailed and fell backwards as the blast of his wife's sudden explosion sounded in his ears and chunks of his wife splattered his face and white wifebeater.

Troy's father shut his eyes for fear of getting parts of his wife in his eyes. The sound of whirring flies started to flood the room, and he began to panic.

He whipped away the filth from his closed eyes, then opened them. He looked at the room, and his eyes went wide. A hurricane of flies surrounded him, buzzing around and making it impossible to hear his own gasp. When he looked toward where he could once see the door to his bedroom, he saw his son, covered from head to toe with flies, start marching towards him.

Troy's father was terrified. He went to backpedal away from his son, but his legs decided they didn't want to operate, and he fell back on his ass again. He backpedaled, kicking against the shaggy carpet of the RV, trying to scooch himself towards the exit so he could run away from the mayhem he still had trouble understanding.

Looking through the mist of flies, he could see his son's eyes leering down at him with a sick pleasure. It was like Troy was enjoying this, enjoying his frightened father scurrying away on the floor, inching towards the door like a maggot in search of the hospitality of a warm corpse.

For a second, a flicker of anger crossed Troy's father's features. He wanted to get up and hurt the boy, instill fear in his son like he usually did, but the rage expired as quickly as it came when Troy took another step towards him.

Backing up as quickly as he could, Troy's father was certifiably scared now. His heart was thumping out of his chest, and goosebumps covered his flesh. His terror was plastered all over his face, his eyes wide, eyebrows raised, and bottom lip trembling uncontrollably. He just wanted for all this to stop, but as he closed his eyes and wished for it to end, the whirring of flies persisted all around him, a buzzing crescendo that sounded like a thousand saws cutting metal all at once.

Troy was now past the bedroom threshold and was looming a few feet away from his father. His steps were slow and methodic, as if the boy underneath the fury of flies was enjoying his father's scared expression.

Troy's father continued to scoot away from Troy, the fear enveloping him causing him to move as slow as a snail.

"Please, don't hurt me," Troy's father said unknowingly under his breath. His voice shook with the uncontrollable trembling coursing through his body. "Please, Troy! Don't hurt me—," his words were cut off when his back bumped into something behind him.

Troy's father felt behind himself, hands searching for the thing he bumped into, hoping to God that what he'd bumped into was simply a table or a seat of some sort, even the wall of the camper would do. Something other than the cold foot that his hand fell upon, which shot shivers down his spine. He slowly turned and looked upwards towards the being looming behind him. His eyes met the malicious glare of a woman whose hate was palpable. Her hate surged through the room like random bolts of electricity from a Tesla coil. At first, the woman was a stranger to him, but the longer he looked at the decomposing being in front of him, the more her features popped out and revealed who she was.

It was the woman he had raped and strangled in the woods.

In a drop of a dime, Troy's father's fear was redirected from his fly covered son to the woman whose raging eyes were on him, staring daggers into his being. Her stare bore into him with a ferocity he had never felt before. The woman's decomposing form was a terrifying site to behold. Flies walked over her flesh, and maggots inched over and sunk into her body. Her skin had a green tinge mixed with a yellowish-white puss color that looked as bad as it smelled. Rot filled Troy's father's senses, and if he weren't paralyzed by fear, he would have vomited right there and then.

She stared down her rapist with eyes that scorched with fury. Troy's father wanted to spare his eyes from the glare, but he couldn't look away from his victim, the one he knew he'd left for dead in the woods.

He couldn't believe this was happening to him. Hell, he couldn't believe something like this could happen in general.

My eyes must be playing a trick on me, he thought.

He was stunned. One minute he was arguing with his bitch of a wife, then the next he was role playing a scene from one of Lucifer's sick fantasies. It seemed impossible, yet here she was before him, flies swarming around her and buzzing with an intensity that made him tremble all over. He realized in a swift, fleeting moment that the roles had reversed. Now, the victim was the monster, and the previous monster was now the prey.

In the split of a second, Troy was on his father, pinning his arms to the ground. Troy's father couldn't see his son's face, but he could see his son's green eyes just under the mask of flies. His eyes were similar to the woman's eyes in the sense that they had malice in them. His son's hate bore into him, and Troy's father realized in that moment that no amount of pleading would make his son let up on his impossible grip.

The woman began taking slow, methodical steps towards Troy's father. Her lips curled upwards into a devilish grin as he attempted to free himself from his son's hold. Unfortunately for him, his son somehow possessed an unfeasible strength that a scrawny child just shouldn't have. Troy's father thrashed around as much as possible, but the hold was unbreakable.

Then the millions of flies filling the camper suddenly changed their flight patterns from sporadic to a mapped course. They flew around the woman with purpose, circling her as she continued to walk closer and closer to the now weeping man before her.

When the woman shrouded in flies came to Troy's father's side, she knelt down to meet his face, which was one of unadulterated fear. When he tried to look away from her deteriorating face, a fury of flies slammed into his cheek, forcing him to turn his face back towards the woman. He attempted to squeeze his eyes shut so he wouldn't have to face her malevolent stare, but the woman pried them open with her decaying fingers.

As he stared into the woman's eyes, he couldn't help but think of his wife. Not once did his wife's face contort with such hatred towards him like the woman's face before him did.

"What do you want from me?" he asked with a quiver.

His question was met with a head tilt from the woman.

"What I want … from you?" she asked, her voice raspy and stretching out like it hadn't been used in ages. "Why, I want you … to suffer!"

Troy's father cowered. Troy was still pinning him to the ground, but he no longer fought against him.

"Please … P-P-Please don't d-d-do this!" he stuttered.

The woman's lips separated, and she gave him a toothy grin, one that revealed the missing front teeth she had swallowed earlier. Blood rushed down her chin, dripping down onto his chest.

"Don't worry," she hissed. "This will be over quick, I promise."

Her gurgled laugh turned into a malicious cackle, then, as soon as it came, it faded in with the increasingly loud droning noise of buzzing flies.

Troy's father screamed as a wave of flies charged him.

The flies entered wherever there was a hole to explore. He could feel every fly crawling all over him, making him itch like crazy. He was still pinned to the floor and unable to swat them away, but he was able to kick his feet out like a mad man. It did little to help him.

The flies crawled into his eyes, ears, mouth, and nose, and there was nothing he could do to stop them.

His anguished cries mixed with the noise of whirring flies, and eventually, the cries coming out of his mouth dissipated altogether until there was nothing but the sounds of flies buzzing around the room. The mass of flies enveloped Troy's father and undulated on top of him.

The body underneath the mass of flies wriggled a bit, but eventually went still. Within twenty minutes, Troy's father was no more.

# About the Author

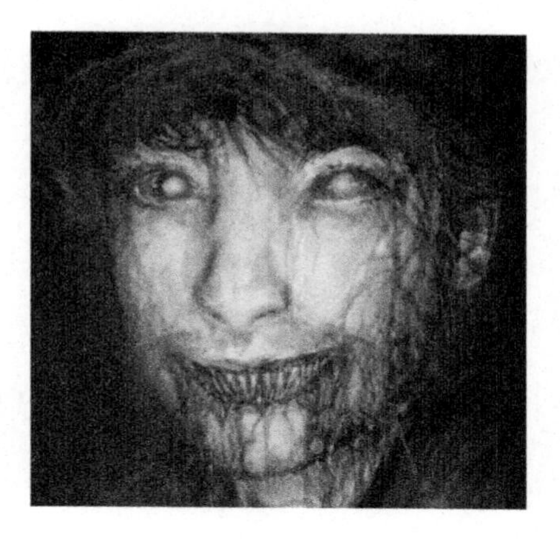

***Nicholas Gray*** is a horror nut that enjoys reading horror, watching horror, and, of course, writing horror. Being a cancer survivor, Nick knows horror and hopes to write an escape from that kind of dread with his. Nick also suffered from a Traumatic Brain injury from a complicated birth. He has persevered through it all, and is surpassing his doctor's expectations, making the naysayers in his life who said that he would never amount to any-thing look very dumb. Some inspirations of Nicholas Gray's are Ronald Kelly, John Wayne Comunale, Jeff Strand, and his little family unit he loves dearly.

Printed in Great Britain
by Amazon